40 SECONDS™

40 SECONDS™

Writer
Jeremy Haun

Artist
Christopher Mitten

Colorist
Brett Weldele

Letterer
Thomas Mauer

Dark Horse Books

DARK HORSE TEAM

President and Publisher
Mike Richardson

Editor
Daniel Chabon

Assistant Editors
Chuck Howitt-Lease and Misha Gehr

Designer
May Hijikuro

Digital Art Technician
Jason Rickerd

Special thanks to
David Steinberger, Chip Mosher, and Bryce Gold

Published by Dark Horse Books
A division of Dark Horse Comics LLC
10956 SE Main Street, Milwaukie, OR 97222

First edition: October 2022
Trade paperback ISBN 978-1-50672-647-2

1 3 5 7 9 10 8 6 4 2

Printed in China

Comic Shop Locator Service: comicshoplocator.com

Library of Congress Cataloging-in-Publication Data

Names: Haun, Jeremy, writer. | Mitten, Christopher (Christopher J.), artist. | Weldele, Brett, colourist. | Mauer, Thomas (Comic book letterer), letterer.
Title: 40 seconds / writer, Jeremy Haun ; artist, Christopher Mitten ; colorist, Brett Weldele ; letterer, Thomas Mauer.
Other titles: Forty seconds
Description: First edition. | Milwaukie, OR : Dark Horse Books, 2022. | Summary: "A science fiction/fantasy adventure about a brave team of science explorers traveling through a series of alien gateways to answer a distress call a galaxy away. They find themselves jumping across the universe through strange and beautiful landscapes only to be hunted by a vast, inexplicably unstoppable and dangerous horde. Amazing truths lie at the final gate. If only they can make it in time.-- Provided by publisher.
Identifiers: LCCN 2022012481 | ISBN 9781506726472 (trade paperback)
Subjects: LCGFT: Science fiction comics. | Fantasy comics. | Graphic novels.
Classification: LCC PN6728.A1356 H38 2022 | DDC 741.5/973--dc23/eng/20220422
LC record available at https://lccn.loc.gov/2022012481

FORTY SECONDS...
PLEASE...
FORTY SECONDS...
HELP US.

FORTY SECONDS...

GOOD MORNING, ONE.

HEY...

WHAT TIME IS IT?

IT IS ZERO FIVE THIRTY HOURS. YOUR ALARM WILL ACTIVATE IN--

ALARM OFF.

OW...

MORNING.
'BOUT TIME. I WAS WONDERING IF WE WERE GONNA HAVE TO DRAG YOU OUT OF BED ON GAME DAY.
HEY-- I'M UP.
THAT SMELLS DELICIOUS. YOU'RE A WIZARD, THREE.
YOU OKAY THERE?
YEAH. I'M FINE. MUST'VE JUST SLEPT WEIRD OR SOMETHING.
OR OVERDID YESTERDAY'S WORKOUT...
DOING IT WRONG THEN.

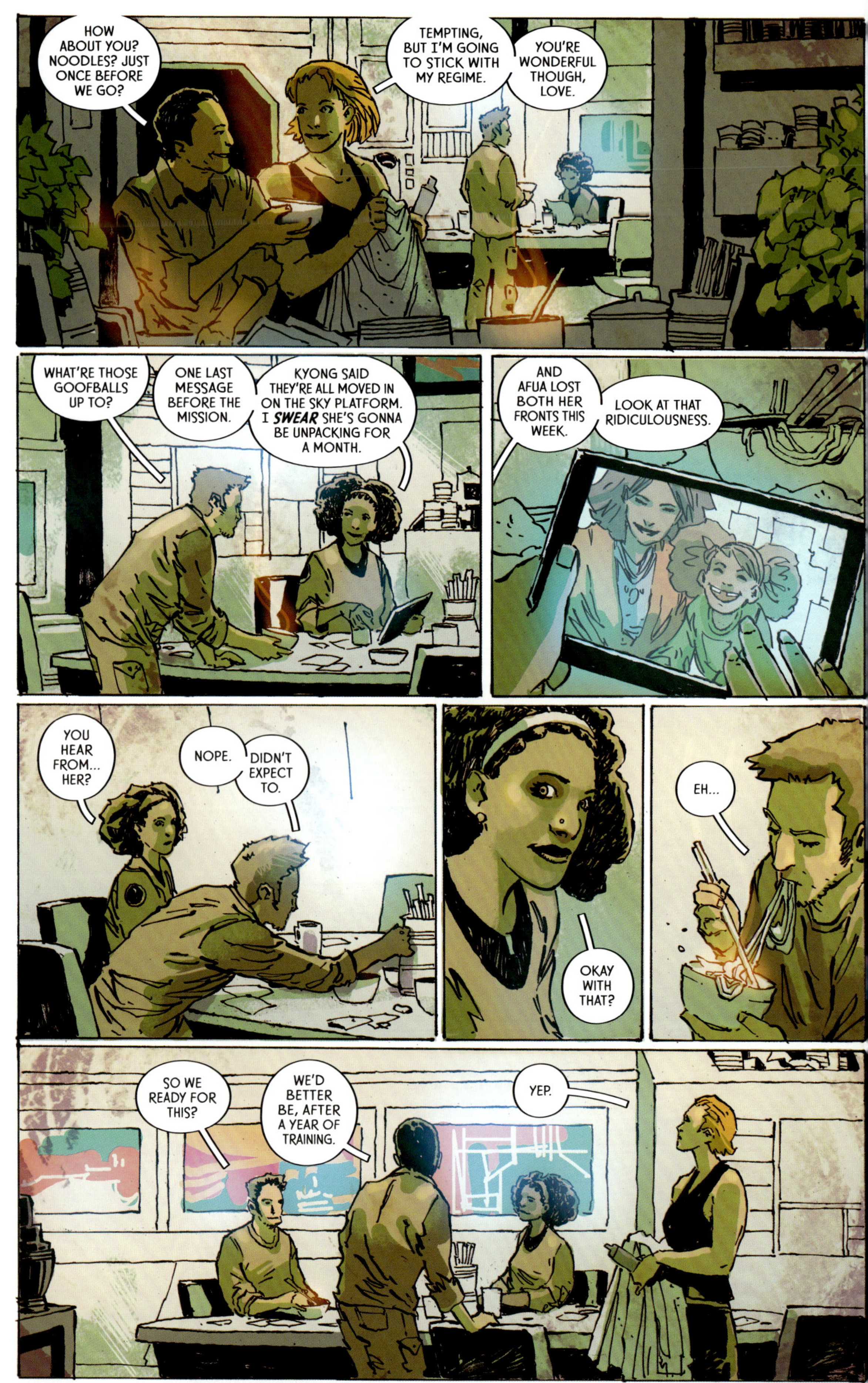
HOW ABOUT YOU? NOODLES? JUST ONCE BEFORE WE GO?
TEMPTING, BUT I'M GOING TO STICK WITH MY REGIME.
YOU'RE WONDERFUL THOUGH, LOVE.
WHAT'RE THOSE GOOFBALLS UP TO?
ONE LAST MESSAGE BEFORE THE MISSION.
KYONG SAID THEY'RE ALL MOVED IN ON THE SKY PLATFORM. I SWEAR SHE'S GONNA BE UNPACKING FOR A MONTH.
AND AFUA LOST BOTH HER FRONTS THIS WEEK.
LOOK AT THAT RIDICULOUSNESS.
YOU HEAR FROM... HER?
NOPE.
DIDN'T EXPECT TO.
OKAY WITH THAT?
EH...
SO WE READY FOR THIS?
WE'D BETTER BE, AFTER A YEAR OF TRAINING.
YEP.

IF ALL GOES WELL, THE PROJECTION IS THIRTY-SIX HOURS START TO FINISH.
WE SET UP, MAKE SURE EVERYTHING IS GOOD, COLLECT DATA, AND THEN HEAD HOME.
EASY PEASY LEMON SQUEEZIE.
I SLEPT LIKE HELL LAST NIGHT.
WEIRD, REPETITIVE DREAMS.
I GET THE JITTERS NIGHT BEFORE JUST ABOUT ANYTHING. ALWAYS HAVE. SLUMBER PARTIES. TRIPS...
DIDN'T SLEEP FOR A **WEEK** BEFORE WE HAD AFUA.
...THEN NOT FOR A ***YEAR*** AFTER.
ALRIGHTY THEN...LET'S SUIT UP.
FINAL BRIEFING IN TWENTY.

FOUR YEARS AGO, WE RECEIVED A BEACON--A DISTRESS SIGNAL. ITS ORIGIN, SOME FOUR MILLION LIGHT YEARS FROM EARTH.
WITHIN THAT BEACON WERE SCHEMATICS FOR ***FORGE GATE TECHNOLOGY.*** IT HAS BROUGHT US TO TODAY.
THIS FORGE GATE TECHNOLOGY ALLOWS US TO JUMP FARTHER THAN WE COULD HAVE EVER IMAGINED. YET IT IS ONLY A PORTION OF THE WAY TO OUR TERMINUS.
AS YOU KNOW, YOU ARE NOT THE FIRST TEAM TO VENTURE THROUGH THIS GATE. WE LOST CONTACT WITH THE FIRST TEAM SEVENTEEN HOURS INTO THE MISSION.
YOU'VE READ THE LOGS. THAT TEAM MADE IT THROUGH A SECOND GATE. THEIR FINAL TRANSMISSIONS WERE FROM A WORLD ONE POINT FOUR MILLION LIGHT YEARS AWAY.

YOU HAVE GONE OVER THE DATA FROM THAT PREVIOUS MISSION. YOU HAVE PREPARED FOR THIS AND EVERY CONCEIVABLE CONTINGENCY.
OFFICER BENNETT...
THANK YOU.
YOU HAVE YOUR MISSION.
IT IS SIMPLE-- YOU WILL TRAVEL THROUGH THIS GATE AND BEYOND. ALONG THE WAY YOU WILL GATHER DATA AT EACH LOCATION. YOU WILL ALSO INVESTIGATE WHAT HAPPENED TO THE PREVIOUS TEAM.
THAT SAID, YOU WILL **NOT** DEVIATE FROM YOUR PRIMARY OBJECTIVE-- REACHING THE TERMINUS.
THAT'S IT, TEAM.
GEAR UP.
BE SAFE AND GODSPEED.

ANNNNND COMMS ARE ONLINE. GIVE ME A CHECK FOR LEVELS.
CHECK.
CHECK.
CHECK.
CHECK.
PERFECT. WE ARE A GO.
OKAY. HERE WE GO.
SHIK
SHIK
SHIK
PLEASE--DO THE HONORS, COLEADER.
THANKS.
LET'S DO THIS...
FORTY SECONDS...
FORTY SECONDS...
FORTY SECONDS...
FORTY SECONDS...

WOW...
YEAH...

I THOUGHT I WAS READY.
NOTHING COULD'VE...
IT'S SO...
...VAST.

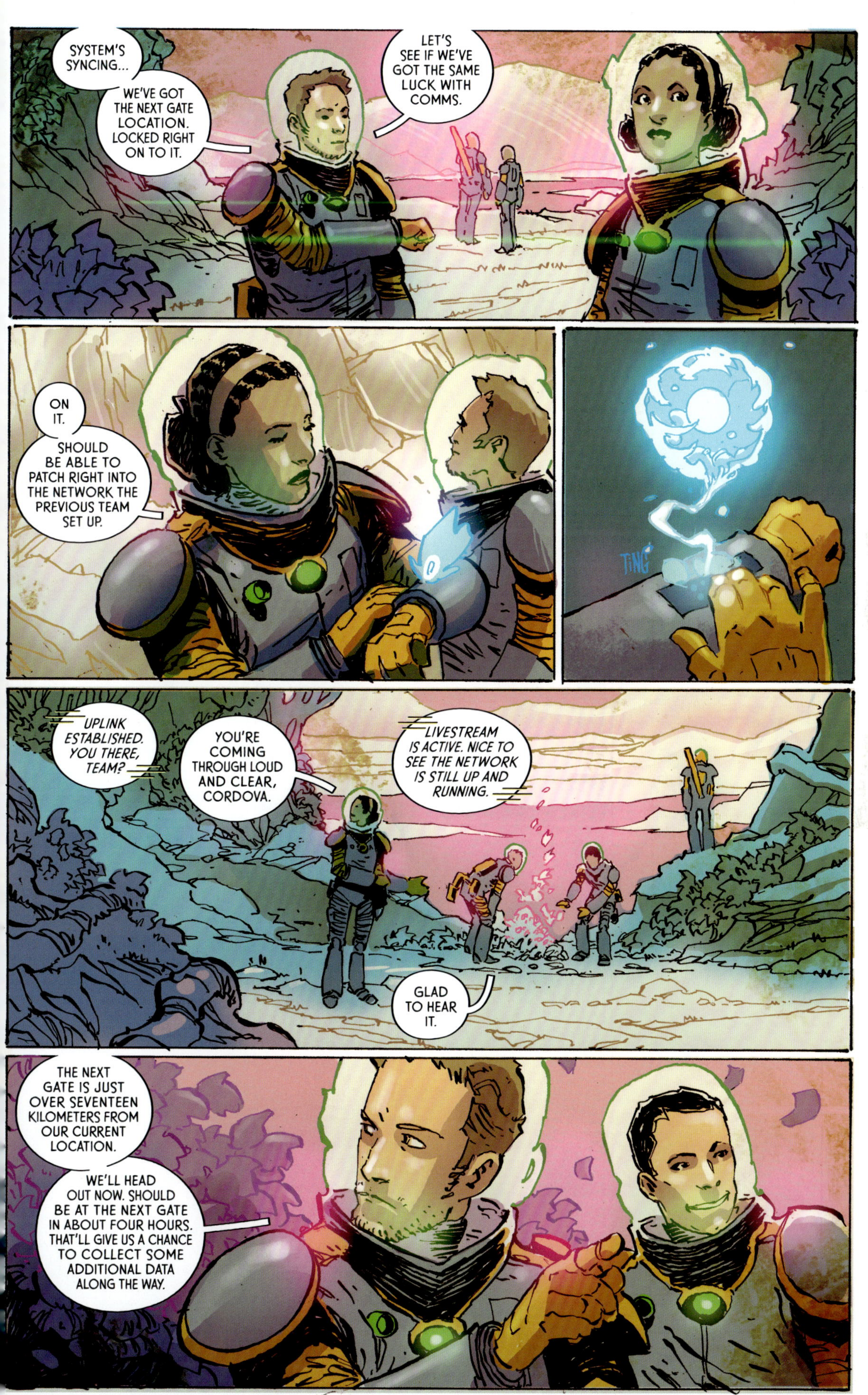

SYSTEM'S SYNCING...
WE'VE GOT THE NEXT GATE LOCATION. LOCKED RIGHT ON TO IT.
LET'S SEE IF WE'VE GOT THE SAME LUCK WITH COMMS.
ON IT.
SHOULD BE ABLE TO PATCH RIGHT INTO THE NETWORK THE PREVIOUS TEAM SET UP.
TING
UPLINK ESTABLISHED. YOU THERE, TEAM?
YOU'RE COMING THROUGH LOUD AND CLEAR, CORDOVA.
LIVESTREAM IS ACTIVE. NICE TO SEE THE NETWORK IS STILL UP AND RUNNING.
GLAD TO HEAR IT.
THE NEXT GATE IS JUST OVER SEVENTEEN KILOMETERS FROM OUR CURRENT LOCATION.
WE'LL HEAD OUT NOW. SHOULD BE AT THE NEXT GATE IN ABOUT FOUR HOURS. THAT'LL GIVE US A CHANCE TO COLLECT SOME ADDITIONAL DATA ALONG THE WAY.

HEY.
HEY...
SO WHAT'RE YOU GONNA DO ONCE WE GET BACK HOME?
HOME?
NOT *GOING* HOME. MY PLACE IS ON THE STATION. FIVE MORE YEARS. HOW IT WORKS.
NOT EVERYONE GETS A SWEET SPOT WITH THEIR FAMILY ON THE SKY PLATFORM OUT OF THIS.
LOOK, I DON'T-- WHAT...
WHAT *IS* THAT?
WHAT'RE YOU...

HEY, GUYS! WE'VE GOT SOMETHING OVER HERE.
IS THIS...
...PART OF A SUIT?
OKAY... THAT'S WEIRD.
LOOKS OLD. LIKE IT'S BEEN THERE FOR A DECADE.
YEAH.
WE NEED TO GET GOING, TEAM.
TWENTY MINUTES TO DARK AND LOOKS LIKE WE'VE GOT A STORM ROLLING IN.
LET'S GET TO THE GATE.
FOUR-- BRING THAT ALONG AND WE'LL SEE IF WE CAN ACCESS ANY DATA FROM IT AFTER WE MAKE THE NEXT JUMP.
DONE.

THERE IT IS!
CORDOVA, WE'VE REACHED THE SECOND GATE WITH MINUTES TO SPARE.
GOT A NASTY STORM ROLLING IN RIGHT BEHIND US. WE GOTTA GET OUT OF HERE.
ROGER THAT, TEAM.
WE'LL LOSE YOU ON OUR END ONCE YOU ACTIVATE THE GATE. RECONNECT AS SOON AS YOU REACH THE NEXT DESTINATION.
BE SAFE.
WILL DO.
HERE WE GO...
FORTY SECONDS...

WAIT...
SHUNK
NO!
FORTY SECONDS...

KEEP HIM ON HIS FEET!
WE'LL NEED TO GET THROUGH THAT GATE AS SOON AS IT ACTIVATES!
DOK DOK DOK DOK
COME *ON,* DAMMIT!
FORTY SECONDS...

GO! GO! GO!
DOK
DOK
DOK
FOUR! COME ON!
NNGGGHHH...
RAAAHHH!

GAAHHH!
COME ON...
COME ON...COME ON...
CAN THEY FOLLOW? ARE THEY COMING THROUGH?!
I DON'T KNOW!
THEY SAID NOTHING ABOUT THIS!

OKAY!
ONE SECOND...
I GOT YOU, MAN!
CHKK
HEY... TH... TH...
GKKNNN...

THOOOM
FORTY SECONDS...
FORTY SECONDS...
COME ON!
COME ON!
I GOT YOU, MAN!
FORTY SECONDS...

GNNNNN...
WHA...
NNNN...

WAIT A
MINUTE...
I...

OW...
ONE!

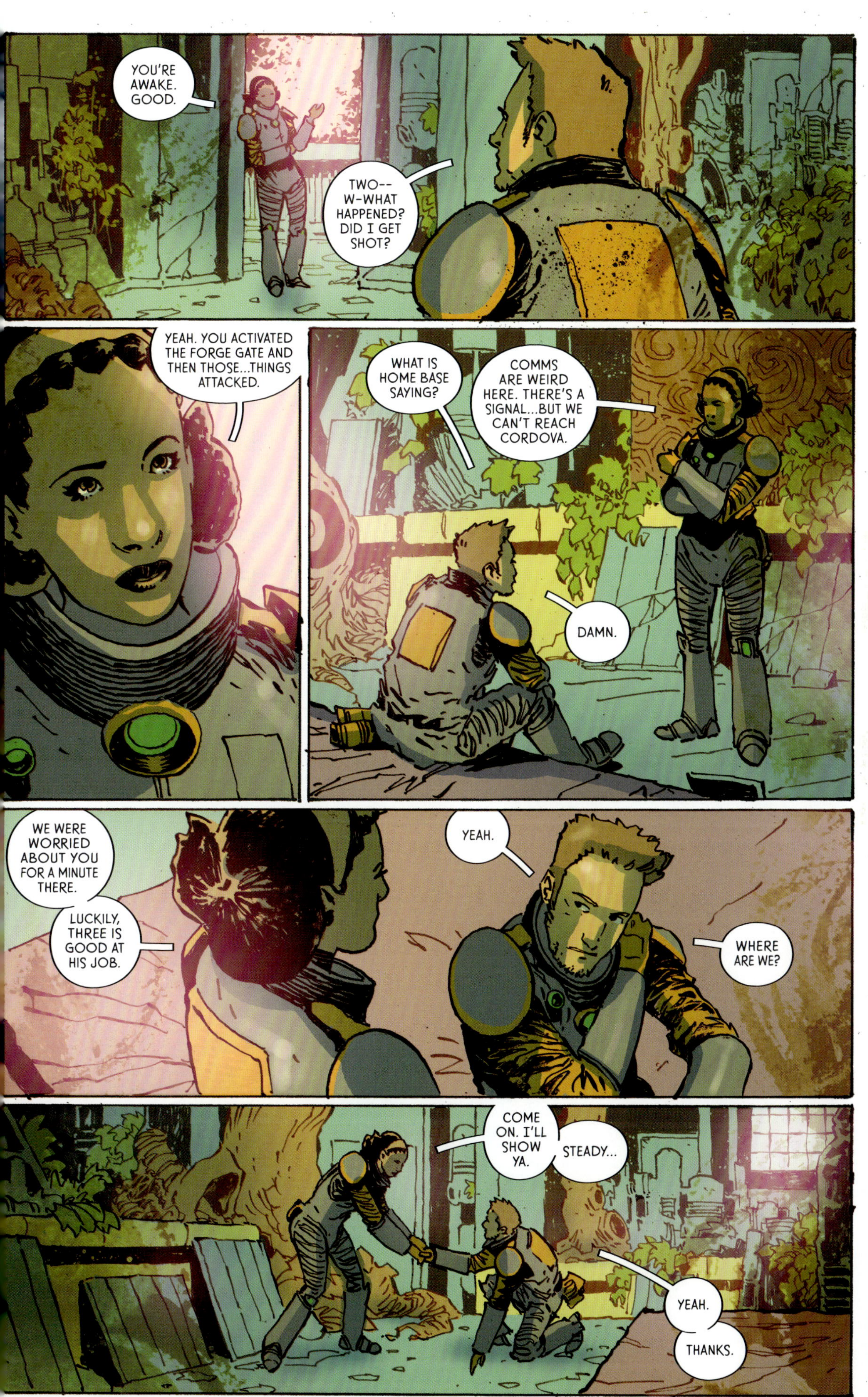
YOU'RE AWAKE. GOOD.
TWO-- W-WHAT HAPPENED? DID I GET SHOT?
YEAH. YOU ACTIVATED THE FORGE GATE AND THEN THOSE...THINGS ATTACKED.
WHAT IS HOME BASE SAYING?
COMMS ARE WEIRD HERE. THERE'S A SIGNAL...BUT WE CAN'T REACH CORDOVA.
DAMN.
WE WERE WORRIED ABOUT YOU FOR A MINUTE THERE.
LUCKILY, THREE IS GOOD AT HIS JOB.
YEAH.
WHERE ARE WE?
COME ON. I'LL SHOW YA.
STEADY...
YEAH.
THANKS.

WE CAME THROUGH HERE. RIGHT IN THE MIDDLE OF THIS CITY.
FEELS LIKE SOMETHING FROM ASIA. IT'S BEAUTIFUL...
...BUT EMPTY.
EMPTY?
LIKE... NOTHING?
NOTHING.
NOTHING AT ALL. IT'S KINDA CREEPY.

WELL, LOOK AT THAT.
I'M GONNA NEED SO MANY SAMPLES...

TIK

OH!

GAAAAAAAHHHHHH...

FOOOOOUUUURRR...
HELP!!

GET DOWN!
FFWWP
THUNK
HUH?
HEY...
A LITTLE GIRL?

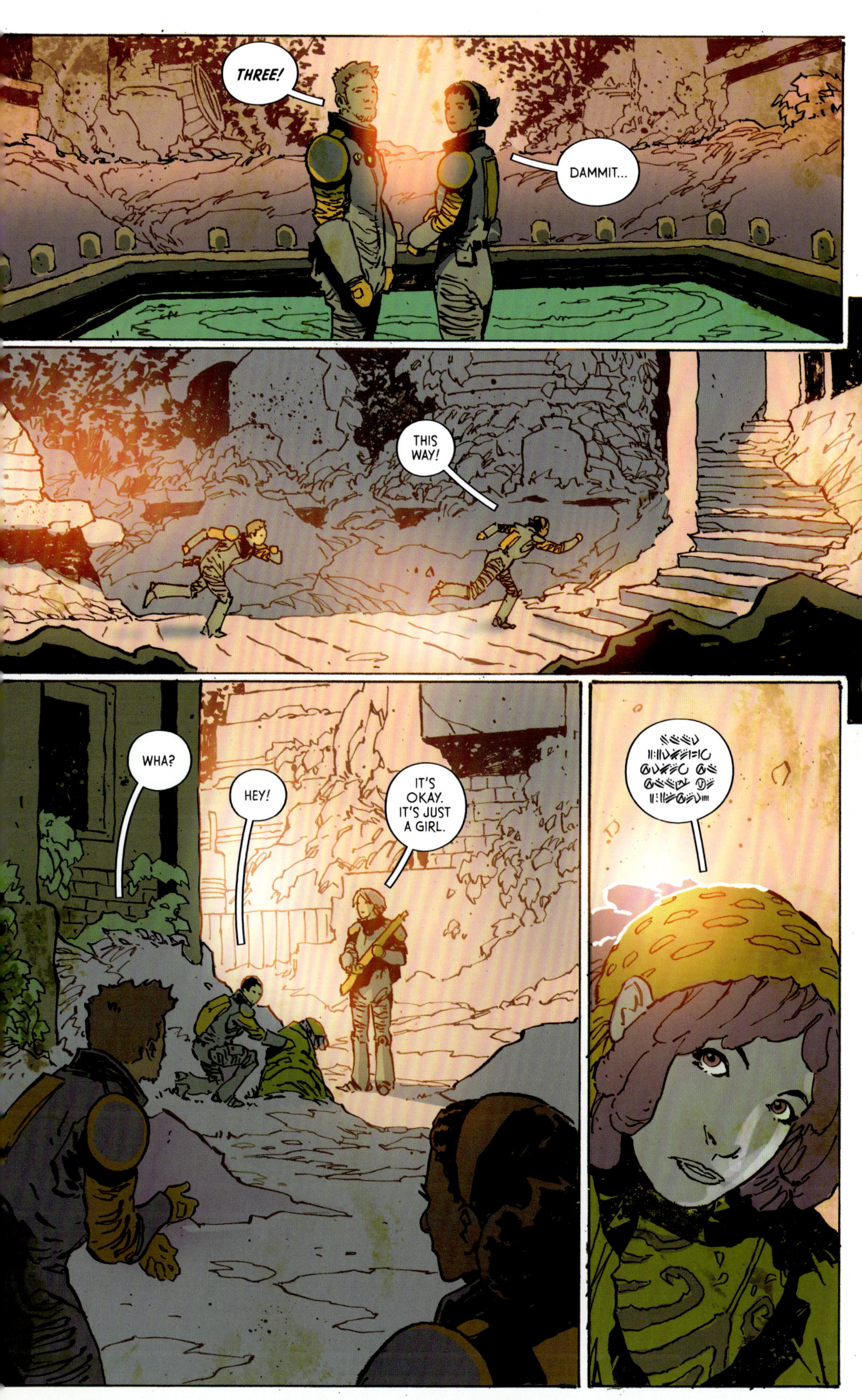
THREE!
DAMMIT...
THIS WAY!
WHA?
HEY!
IT'S OKAY. IT'S JUST A GIRL.

HEY. ARE YOU OKAY, SWEETIE?
HERE-- THIS'LL HELP.
LIKE THIS.
THERE YOU GO.
YOU CAN UNDERSTAND ME NOW, CAN'T YOU?
YES. I CAN UNDERSTAND.
YOU.
YOU CAN'T TOUCH THE WATER. IT IS BAD-- *WRONG...*

DAMMIT...
NO!
PLEASE! NO!
PLEASE!
IT'S JUST US. IT'S JUST US.
HE'S ALL I HAVE.
NO, THEY'RE OKAY.
THEY DIDN'T TOUCH THE WATER.
OKAY. WE'RE ALL GOOD HERE.
LET'S... JUST GET INSIDE AND FIGURE THIS ALL OUT A BIT.
YEAH. LET'S DO THAT.

WE LIVED HERE FOR GENERATIONS ON END. WE WERE HAPPY. AT PEACE.
THEN, ONE DAY, ***THEY*** CAME...LIKE A SWARM.
THEY TAINTED THE WATER. THOSE WHO TOUCHED IT CHANGED, AND THEN THEY WERE GONE. EVERYONE.
EVERYONE EXCEPT US.
HOW LONG AGO WAS THAT?
TWO YEARS NOW...MAYBE MORE?
IT'S HARD TO EVEN TELL ANYMORE. WE ONLY WORK TO SURVIVE.

WE HAVE SEEN OTHERS COME FROM TIME TO TIME. WE STAY AWAY. ALWAYS STAY AWAY.
THEY ACTIVATE THE GATE AND THEN THE SWARM COMES.
WE HIDE. WE SURVIVE.
WE--
COUGH COUGH COUGH
UNCLE...
ARE YOU OKAY?
I WILL BE FINE...
HEY, LET ME TAKE A LOOK AT YOU.
MAYBE I CAN HELP.

YOU ALL FINDING ANYTHING?
I JUST DON'T GET IT. WE SHOULD BE ABLE TO AT LEAST ACCESS THE DATA CORE ON THIS THING.
IT'S WEIRD, THOUGH... WE GET NOTHING.
THERE'S A NAME TAG ON IT, TOO.
DID THE PREVIOUS TEAM DO THAT?
BARNES
I... DON'T KNOW.
WEIRD.
YEAH.
AS SOON AS WE GET COMMS BACK UP, I WANT TO ASK ABOUT THIS. SOMETHING SEEMS OFF.

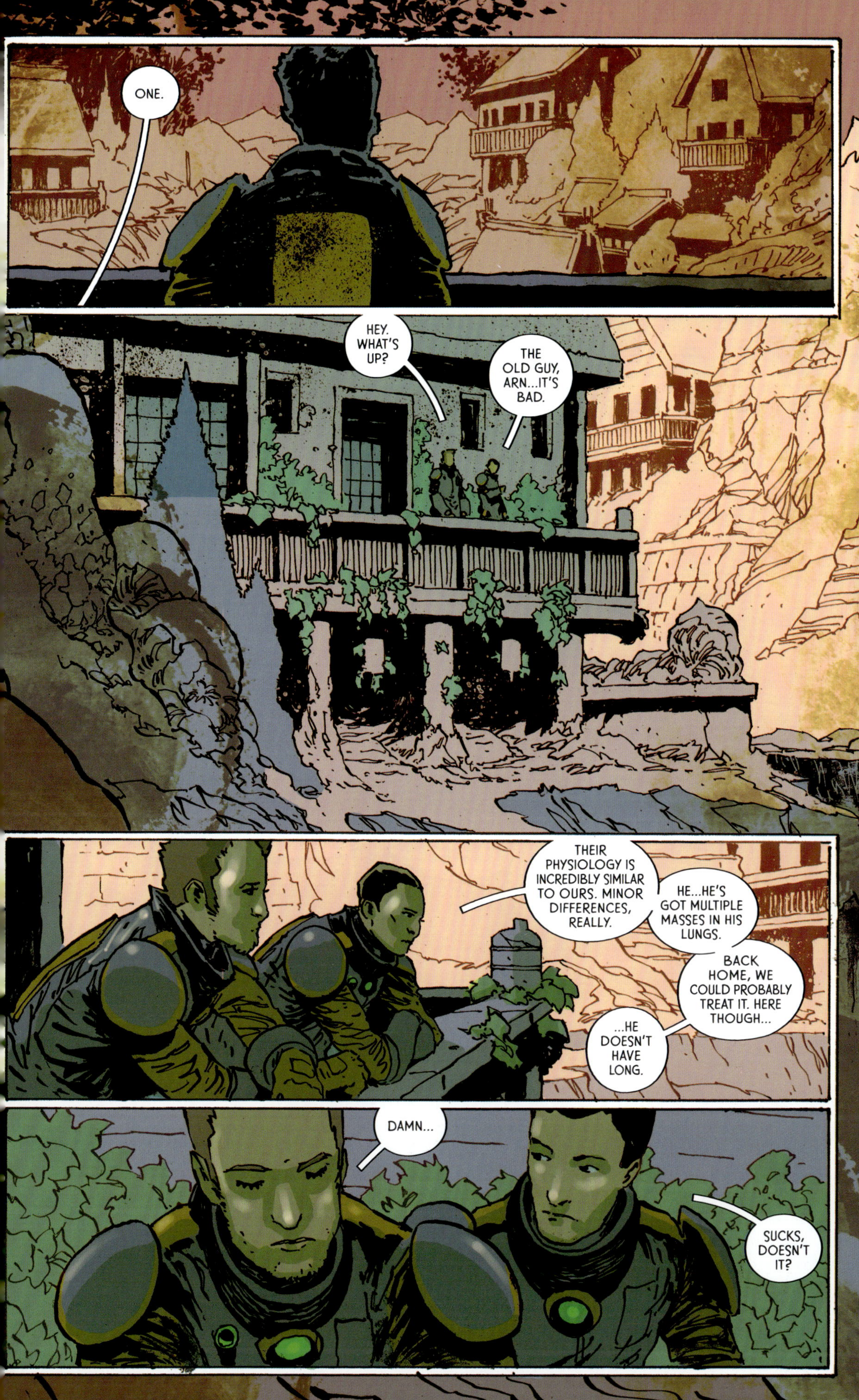
ONE.
HEY. WHAT'S UP?
THE OLD GUY, ARN...IT'S BAD.
THEIR PHYSIOLOGY IS INCREDIBLY SIMILAR TO OURS. MINOR DIFFERENCES, REALLY.
HE...HE'S GOT MULTIPLE MASSES IN HIS LUNGS.
BACK HOME, WE COULD PROBABLY TREAT IT. HERE THOUGH...
...HE DOESN'T HAVE LONG.
DAMN...
SUCKS, DOESN'T IT?

SHE LOOKS COZY.
YEAH. TWO IS GREAT. SHE HAS A DAUGHTER OF HER OWN BACK HOME.
SHE LIKES YOUR FRIEND.
THIS HAS BEEN A STRANGE DAY.
FOR YOU AND ME BOTH, BUDDY.
YOU WERE INJURED WHEN YOU GOT HERE. BADLY.
YEAH. IT'S BETTER, THOUGH. OUR MEDICINE IS...
...REALLY GOOD.
YOUR FRIEND, THE FUNNY ONE, TOLD YOU I'M SICK THEN.
I CAN FEEL IT--MY FADING. I'VE KNOWN FOR A WHILE NOW.
IT'S PART OF MY PATH. STILL-- MY ONLY CONCERN IS FOR GAIA. SHE WILL BE THE LAST OF US IN THIS SAD WASTED LAND.
TOMORROW YOU WILL ACTIVATE THE PORTAL. WHEN YOU DO, THE DARK SWARM WILL COME FOR YOU.
BEFORE ALL OF THIS, I WAS PROTECTORATE-- THE WARRIOR CLASS.
TAKE US WITH YOU-- HELP THE GIRL AND I CAN HELP.
OKAY.
TELL ME YOUR PLAN.

THOOOM

FORTY SECONDS...

WAIT...

THWOOOOOOSH!
FWIP!
FORTY SECONDS...
GO GO GO!

GAH!
AWWW... WHAT THE HELL, MAN?!
THIS IS HORRIBLE!
CHECKING FOR THE NEXT GATE LOCATION...
CAN WE ESTABLISH COMMS?
GOD I HOPE THIS WORKS HERE!
TING

BZZZT
UPLINK ESTABLISHED! CAN YOU HEAR ME, TEAM?!
CORDOVA! Y-YES!
GOOD! WHAT THE HELL HAPPENED? WE LOST YOU RIGHT BEFORE YOU WENT THROUGH THE GATE.
BZZT
WE'VE BEEN GETTING SIGNAL, BUT NO DATA AT ALL FOR THE LAST FOURTEEN HOURS!
CORDOVA, SOMETHING'S WRONG.
WE JUMPED RIGHT INTO THE MIDDLE OF A FULL-ON BLIZZARD.
WE NEED TO GET TO THE NEXT GATE-- SOME SHELTER AT LEAST...
BZZZT
LIVESTREAM IS ACTIVE, TEAM.
WAIT... YOU'VE GOT TWO MORE SUITS ONLINE.
WHAT BZZZT GOING ON?
WE FOUND TWO SURVIVORS. WE BROUGHT THEM ALONG WITH US...
WAIT-- TWO...WHAT DO YOU MEAN... SURVIVORS? I...
KKRRRHHHKK
WHAT THE HELL WAS THAT?
CORDOVA, WE'VE GOT SOME KIND OF SEISMIC ACTIVITY.
THIS PLACE IS NOT STABLE!
GET TO SHELTER. NOW!
CONTACT US AS SOON AS YOU FIND A SAFE SPACE!
KKRRRROUUGHHH

I DON'T LIKE THIS!
COME ON! IT'S THE ONLY WAY!
KKKRRRKHHHHKKKK
AAAHH!
KKRRRRKK
NO!

TWO!
NNNNNN!
NO NO
NO NO
NO!
NOOOOOOO!

SHE'S JUST... GONE...
I KNOW.
I KNOW...
I WAS SUCH AN ASSHOLE TO HER...
SHE...
CORDOVA! COME IN!
FWOOSH
BZZZT ONE! WE'RE HAVING TROUBLE WITH THE LIVESTREAM!
...DELAY. CAN'T SEE ANYTHING!
WHAT-- BZZZT --GOING ON?
DAMMIT...
WE... WE LOST TWO.
WHAT?
SHE'S GONE...

BZZZT
HOW DID THAT HAPPEN?
SHE FELL.
THE STORM IS BAD. THERE WAS SOME KIND OF SEISMIC EVENT.
WE TRIED.
FOUR TRIED...
TWO JUST... FELL.
HOW FAR ARE-- BZZZT --FROM THE NEXT FORGE GATE?
WAIT... WHAT? I JUST SAID WE LOST TWO!
UNDERSTOOD.
BZZZT BUT THE MISSION STILL STANDS. YOU HAVE TO BZZZT GET TO THE NEXT GATE.
YOU-- BZZZT
CORDOVA?
BZZZT BZZZZT
CORDOVA!
DAMMIT!
KKSSSHHH

UNNNNNNHH...
UNCLE!
ARN-- I GOTCHA, BUDDY.
IT'S OKAY. IT'S GONNA BE OKAY.
PLEASE, PLEASE! UNCLE...
NO...NO... FINE.
I'M FINE...
COME ON, MAN-- JUST GIVE ME A SECOND HERE.
COUGH COUGH COUGH
THREE?
OKAY...
WE'VE GOTTA GO.

WHAT IF THEY...
WE GOT THIS.
DO IT.
THOOOM
WHAT...
FORTY SECONDS..
FORTY SECONDS...
WHAT ARE THEY DOING?
WHERE ARE THE REST...
FOUR!
WE GOTTA GO NOW!
FORTY SECONDS...

OHTHANKGAWD--
--NO ICE.
IT'S... BEAUTIFUL.
NOW WE JUST NEED TO FIGURE OUT HOW TO GET DOWN...

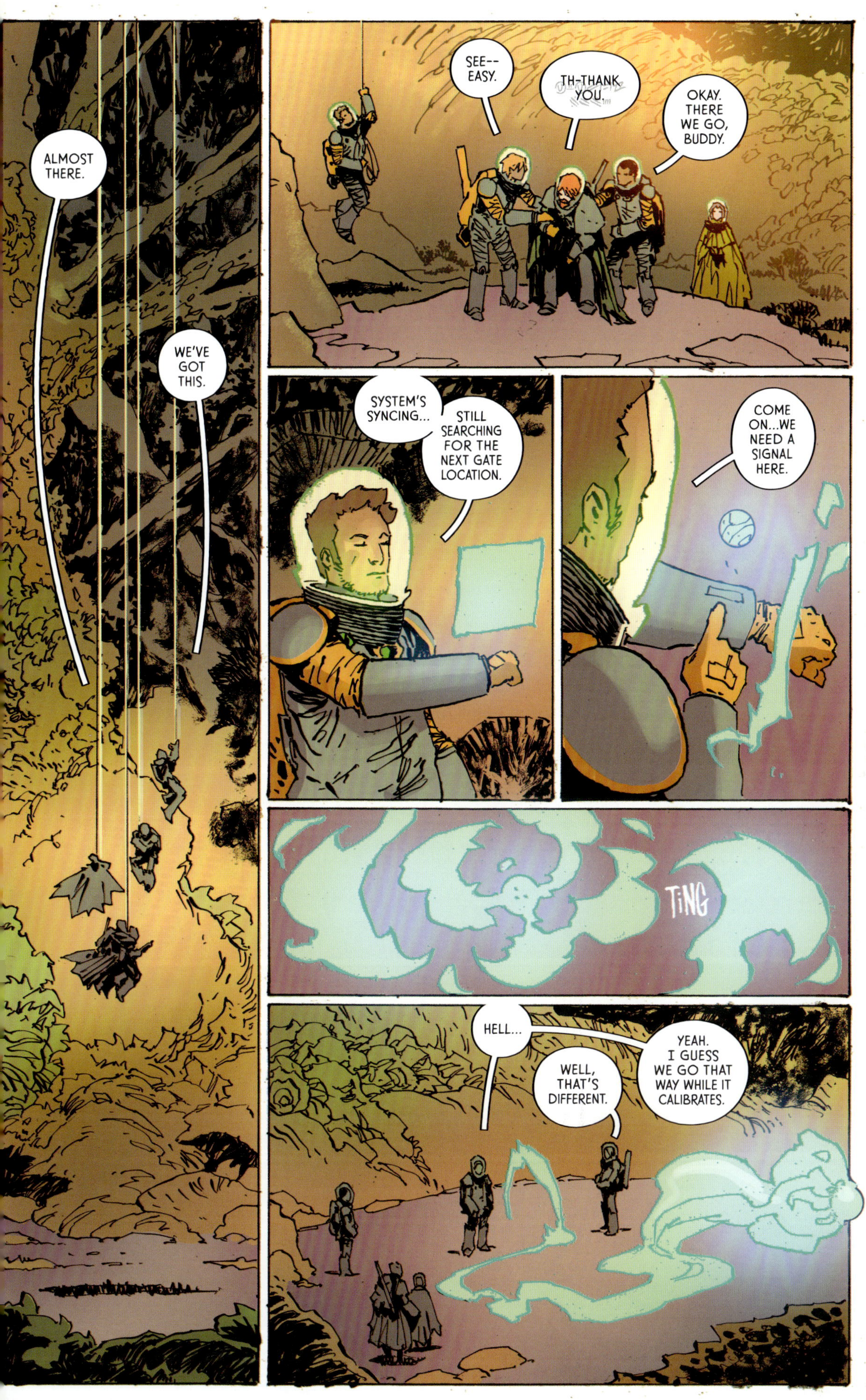
ALMOST THERE.
WE'VE GOT THIS.
SEE-- EASY.
TH-THANK YOU.
OKAY. THERE WE GO, BUDDY.
SYSTEM'S SYNCING...
STILL SEARCHING FOR THE NEXT GATE LOCATION.
COME ON...WE NEED A SIGNAL HERE.
TING
HELL...
WELL, THAT'S DIFFERENT.
YEAH. I GUESS WE GO THAT WAY WHILE IT CALIBRATES.

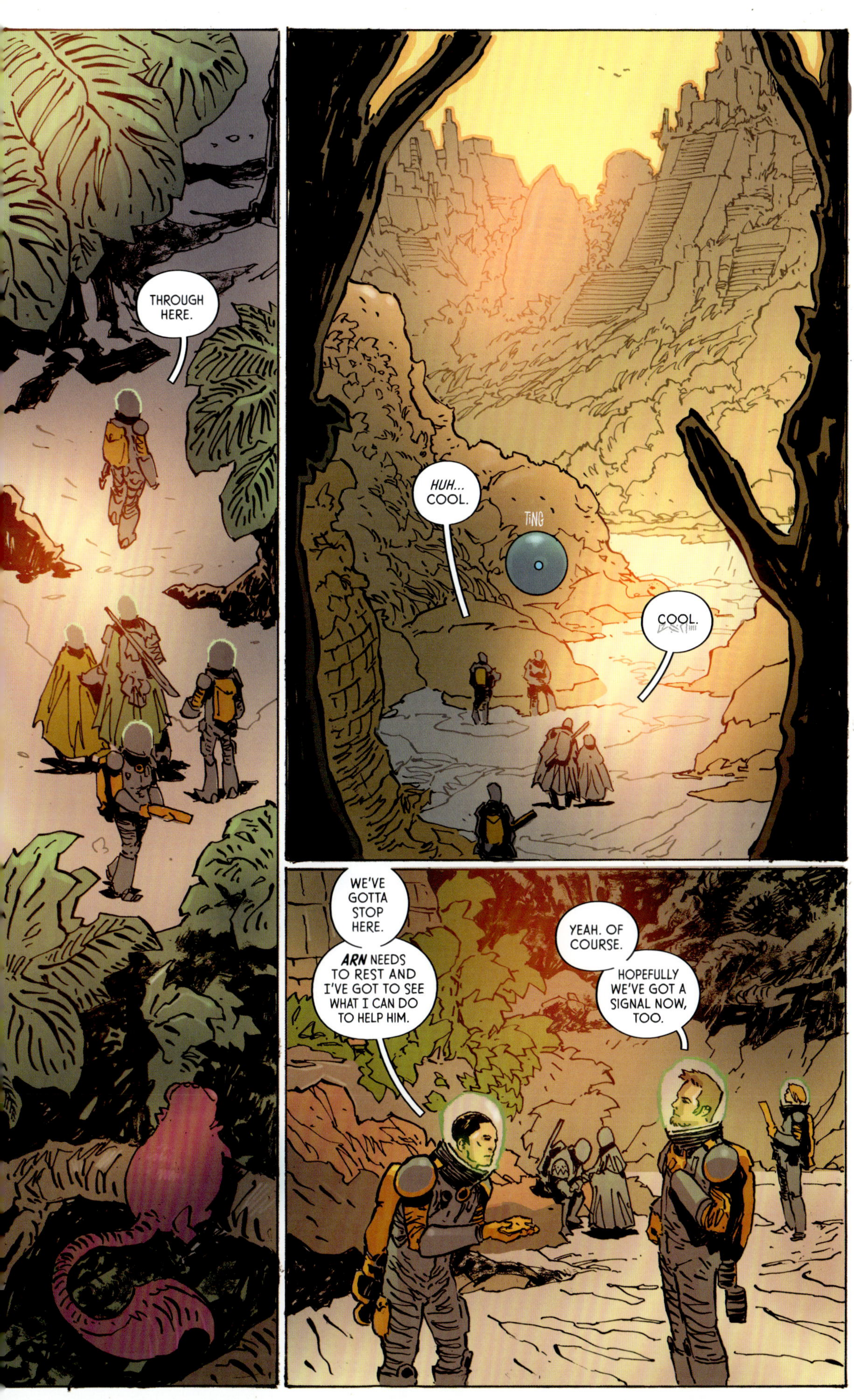
THROUGH HERE.
HUH... COOL.
TING
COOL.
WE'VE GOTTA STOP HERE.
ARN NEEDS TO REST AND I'VE GOT TO SEE WHAT I CAN DO TO HELP HIM.
YEAH. OF COURSE.
HOPEFULLY WE'VE GOT A SIGNAL NOW, TOO.

THERE YOU GO, BUDDY.
THAT'S BETTER.
HUH.
OXYGEN LEVELS ARE... FANTASTIC HERE.
I'VE NEVER SEEN AIR THIS CLEAN.
I GOT YA.
YOU'RE ALL GOOD.
THANK YOU, FRIEND.
OHH, THAT'S SO GOOD.
I DIDN'T LIKE IT IN THERE.
YEAH. I'M RIGHT THERE WITH YOU.
YOU'RE PRETTY MUCH REBREATHING STRAIGHT FARTS IN THESE THINGS.

TING
OH-- HEY!
WE'VE GOT A LOCK ON THE GATE.
IT'S...
...UP THERE.
BZZZT
CORDOVA?
UPLINK ESTABLISHED.
ONE, THIS IS A PRIVATE LINE GOING TO JUST YOU.
OKAY...
WE NEED YOU TO STEP AWAY FROM THE REST OF THE GROUP FOR A MINUTE.
YEAH...I... GUESS...
I'LL BE RIGHT BACK.
STAY CLOSE.
DEFINITELY.

ALL RIGHT-- WHAT'S GOING ON?
WHY ARE YOU JUST TALKING TO ME?
BZZZT
--WE NEED A CLEAR ASSESSMENT OF THE SITUATION, ONE.
SOMETHING IS WRONG. COMMUNICATIONS ARE NOT WORKING AS THEY SHOULD.
LIVE-STREAMS ARE...SPOTTY AT BEST.
ALSO... WE NEED TO TALK ABOUT TWO.
YEAH...
ONE.
BENNETT? WHAT'RE YOU... THIS ISN'T PROTOCOL.
THAT DOESN'T MATTER RIGHT NOW.
BZZT --YOU NEED TO TELL ME EVERYTHING THAT HAS HAPPENED.

THERE YOU GO.
THAT'S BETTER.
THANK YOU.
GAIA, CAN YOU SEE FOR ME IF FOUR WANTS SOME WATER, PLEASE?
I CAN.
WORSE?
YEAH.
A LOT?
Y-YEAH...
THIS'LL HELP.
BUT YOU NEED TO BE CAREFUL.
YOU'LL FEEL BETTER, BUT IT WON'T LAST LONG, OKAY?
OH...THAT... IS BETTER.
MUCH.
GOOD.
JUST TAKE IT SLOW. WE DON'T HAVE MUCH OF IT.

HELLO.
HEY, GAIA.
DRINK?
THANK YOU.
YOU'RE SAD.
YEAH. I'M SAD.
ABOUT TWO. SHE WAS NICE.
SHE WAS YOUR FRIEND...
NO.
SHE WASN'T REALLY MY FRIEND.
AND THAT'S MY FAULT.
SHE WAS NICE.
I SHOULD'VE BEEN BETTER. SHOULD'VE BEEN A FRIEND.
I-- OH...

QI
OH!
CAREFUL...
SCANNING IT...
NO RADIATION OR TOXINS.
STILL, BE CAREFUL.
QI
QI
QI.

WAIT, BENNETT... WHAT DO YOU MEAN?
THIS MISSION CANNOT BE COMPROMISED.
WE LOST **TWO.**
I DON'T CARE WHO THEY ARE, I'M **NOT** LEAVING GAIA AND ARN BEHIND.
WE PROMISED TO **HELP** THEM.
YOU HAVE YOUR ORDERS, ONE.
BZZT YOU WILL LEAVE THE ALIENS AND JUMP THROUGH THE NEXT FORGE GATE...
HUH...
WHAT'S THAT?
THIS CONVERSATION IS OVER.
IF YOU WANT TO TALK TO ME, YOU TALK TO THE WHOLE GROUP.
BZZT --WAIT-- WHERE ARE YOU?
WAIT! GIVE ME--
DEET

WHAT... IS...
WAIT...
NO...

THIS CAN'T BE...
DAMMIT.
OH...
AHHH...
SCKRAAA
AAAAHHHH!

HAHAHAHA!
DO IT AGAIN.
YOU REALLY SHOULDN'T HAVE GIVEN HER THE CANDY...
HUUUUUSH, YOU.
THEY'RE HERE!
WHAT?
THEY'RE ALREADY HERE!
THOOOM THOOOM THOOOM
WHAT?!
GET TO THE GATE NOW!
DON'T WAIT FOR ME!
GO GO GO!
FOUR?
GO!

COME ON, YOU IDIOT...
GOOOOOOOOOOO!
NO! UNCLE!
PLEASE, COME ON!
WE GOT YOU!
NO...
I--I CAN STILL H-HELP.

GIVE IT TO ME.
M-MEDICINE. ALL OF IT.
THANK YOU...
NONONO, UNCLE!
IT IS MY PATH.
I LOVE YOU, LITTLE BIRD.
ALWAYS.
NNNNN
GO. PLEASE!
KEEP HER SAFE...
I AM ARN OF THE PROTECTORATE. LAST OF MY KIND.
I STAND SO THAT OTHERS CAN LIVE.
I STAND--

THOOOM
YAAAHH!
DOK DOK
DOK DOK
FORTY SECONDS...
FORTY SECONDS...
UNCLE!
FORTY SECONDS...
GNNNHH!
GO!

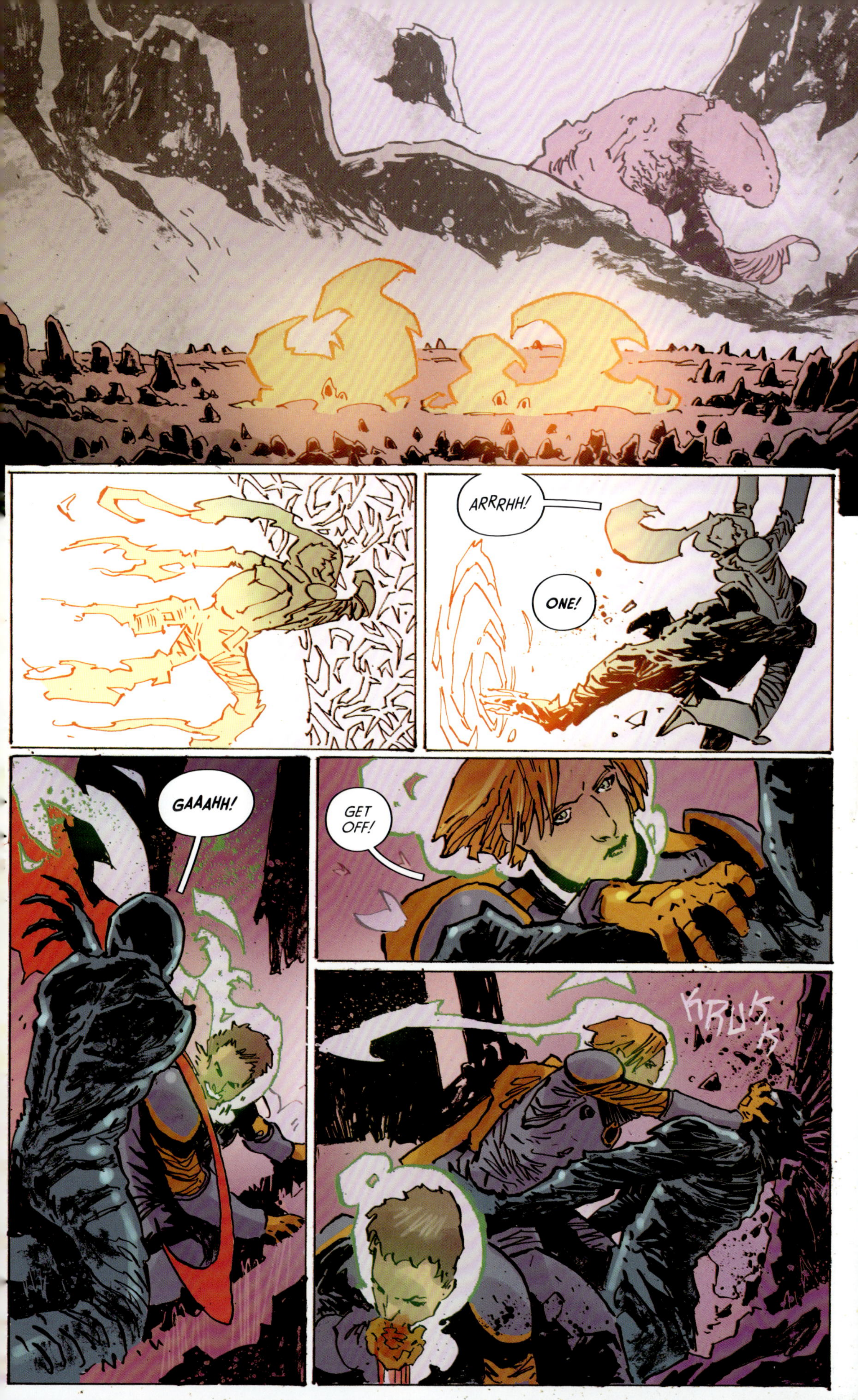
ARRRHH!
ONE!
GAAAHH!
GET OFF!
KRUKK

NNNNGHGH
RRRRRRRGH!
WHAT...
THE HELL?
RRRRRGGH

WHAT...

GRRRAAAAAHHHH
AARRGH!
RAAAAGGHH
YOOOOOOOUUUU

RRAHAHAHAHAHA!
SHHUNKK
OHMYGOD...

I-- WAIT...
TWO?

THOOOM
COMING...
WE NEED TO GO. NOW.
FOLLOW ALONG IF YOU WANT TO SURVIVE THIS.
WAIT A MINUTE... WHAT'S EVEN...
I-I DON'T KNOW.
HEY...
HEY... WAS THAT...
FOLLOW.
CLOSE.

I DON'T KNOW ABOUT THIS.
IT'S *TWO.*
AND... DAMN...
I HAVE TO KNOW.
WAIT-- *ONE!*
WHAT IF QI CAN'T SWIM?
I--
OH!
I'M COMING, QI!
THIS IS SO WEIRD...
YEAH. YOU CAN SAY THAT AGAIN.
DO WE GO?
TOGETHER.

OH, WOW...
THIS IS BEAUTIFUL.
QI QI QI
COME ON. WE'VE GOT A WAYS TO GO.
GO...

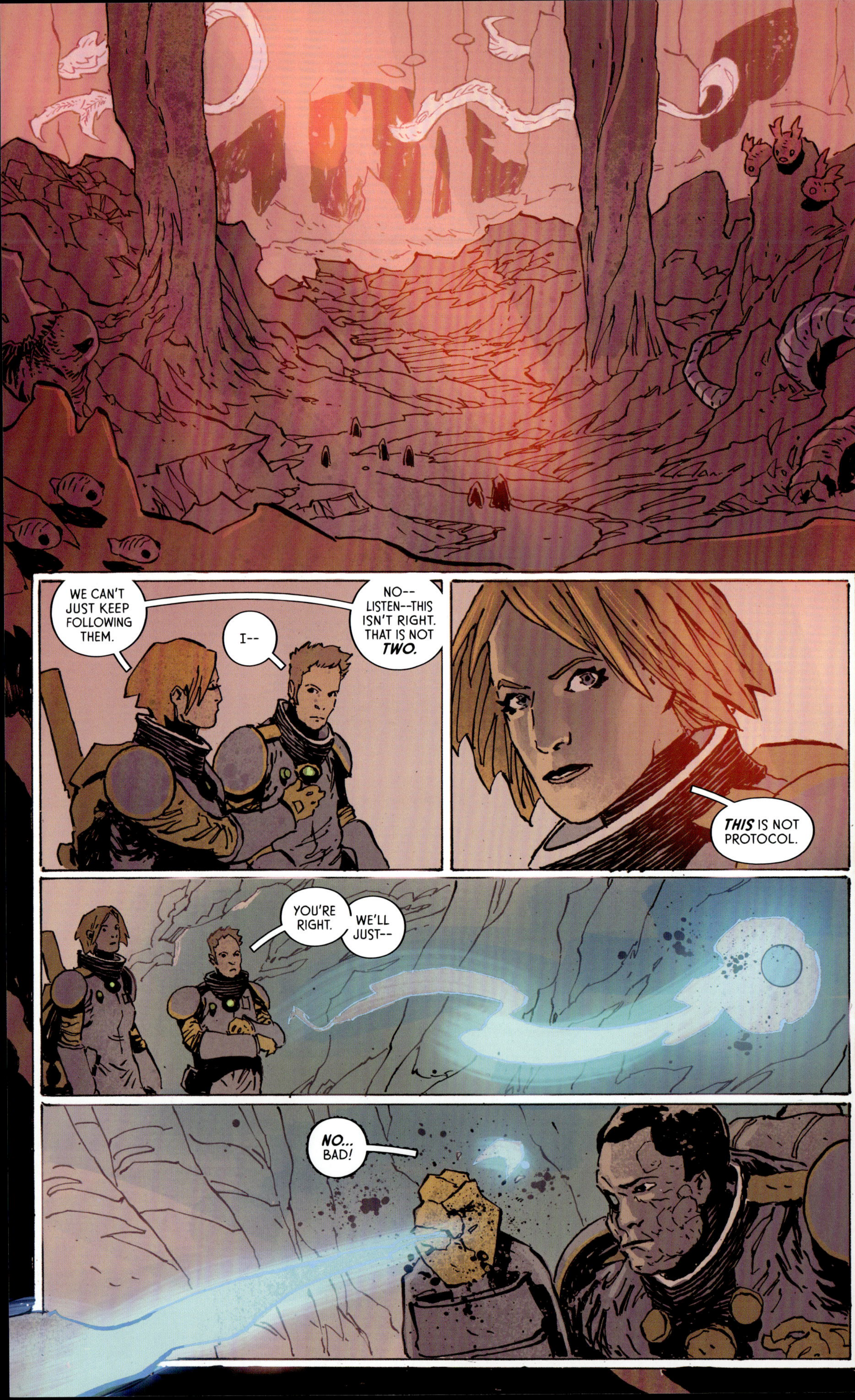

WE CAN'T JUST KEEP FOLLOWING THEM.
I--
NO-- LISTEN--THIS ISN'T RIGHT. THAT IS NOT **TWO.**
THIS IS NOT PROTOCOL.
YOU'RE RIGHT.
WE'LL JUST--
NO... BAD!

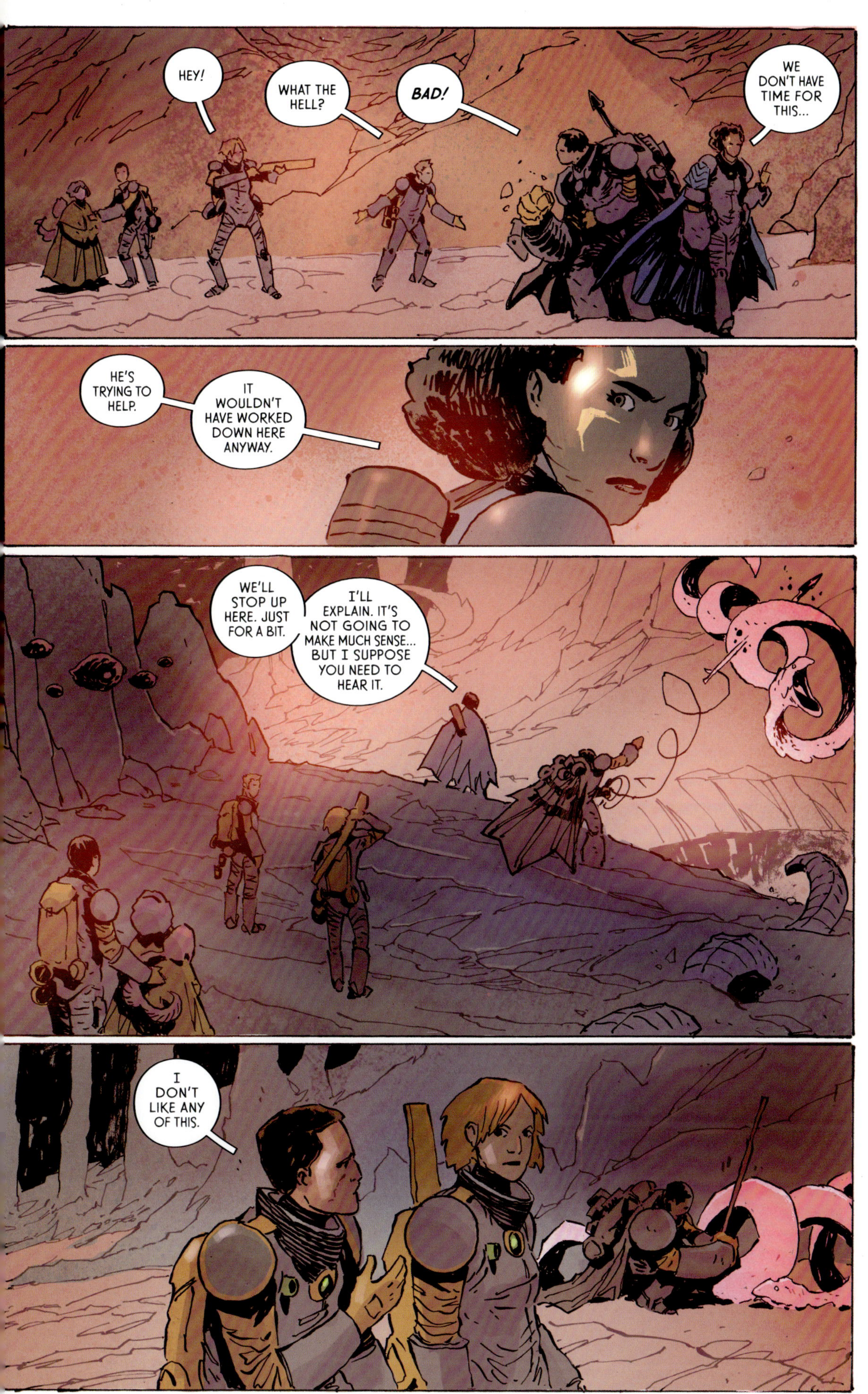
HEY!
WHAT THE HELL?
BAD!
WE DON'T HAVE TIME FOR THIS...
HE'S TRYING TO HELP.
IT WOULDN'T HAVE WORKED DOWN HERE ANYWAY.
WE'LL STOP UP HERE. JUST FOR A BIT.
I'LL EXPLAIN. IT'S NOT GOING TO MAKE MUCH SENSE... BUT I SUPPOSE YOU NEED TO HEAR IT.
I DON'T LIKE ANY OF THIS.

I'M NOT HER--YOUR TWO.
YOU GET THAT, RIGHT?
WE COME FROM THE SAME PLACE-- HAVE THE SAME MEMORIES.
I HAD A DAUGHTER-- A WIFE. BUT... THEY WEREN'T REALLY MINE.
NO MORE THAN ANY OF THE THINGS YOU FEEL AND REMEMBER ARE YOURS.
NO. I DON'T BELIEVE IT.
I JUST DON'T...
COME ON...LOOK AT HER.
LOOK AT...I...
THAT... ME...
TELL US.
EVERYTHING.

IT'S EASIER IF I SHOW YOU.
SOME ARE MINE. SOME ARE FROM THE DATA LOGS FROM OTHER... GENERATIONS.
BUT IT'S ALMOST ALWAYS THE SAME.
THEY SEND US THROUGH THE FORGE GATE-- FOLLOWING AFTER A TEAM THAT WAS...LOST.
"LOST"...
WHAT'S YOUR NAME?
FOUR. YOU KNOW THAT.
NO. YOUR REAL NAME. WHAT IS IT?
I...
REAL NAME? WHAT DOES THAT EVEN...
...I'M FOUR--

BARNES.
THAT WAS YOUR NAME. THE FIRST TIME.
WHAT'RE YOU SAYING?
BARNES
A TEAM OF FOUR SPECIALLY TRAINED AND QUALIFIED EXPLORERS WERE SENT THROUGH FORGE GATE TECHNOLOGY, SENT TO US FROM ANOTHER GALAXY.
THAT TEAM HAD NAMES. LIVES. FAMILIES.
THEY WERE US.
KATHERINE BARNES.
PARK SOO-HYUN.
ETHAN FORSTER.
PAAAARK.
PARK...
THEY WERE LOST.
SO CORDOVA-- WHOEVER WAS THERE THEN-- MADE MORE OF US.
AND SENT US AGAIN. AND AGAIN. AND AGAIN.

THIS CAN'T...
THIS CAN'T BE REEEEEEAL.
DO YOU EVER WONDER WHY YOU HAVE THOSE DREAMS? WHY YOU FEEL THINGS AND REMEMBER THINGS?
AND WHY THERE ARE HOLES IN OTHER PLACES? MEMORIES YOU JUST CAN'T QUITE GRASP...
AWW, BABE...
QI
IT'S OKAY...IT'S OKAY.
WHAT HAPPENED TO THEM, THEN?
THE FIRST TEAM?
THE FIRST... US?
THEY LOST SIGNAL WITH CORDOVA-- MADE IT FARTHER THAN ANYONE THOUGHT.
THEY WERE... ***EXPOSED*** TO SOMETHING. A DARK ICHOR.
IT ***CHANGED*** THEM.
KKKHHSSSHHH
IT-- NO...

DAMMIT... IT'S TIME...
WE'VE GOTTA GO.
H-- WHOA... *WHOA!*
TIME!
WOW...
HURRY! THIS WAY!

OKAY...
OKAY. TIME.
YEAH. TIME.
GO!
THANK YOU, MY FRIEND.
KEEP THEM. SAFE.
PARK. TIME.
SHUNK
GOODBYE...

UP THE LINE! QUICK AS YOU CAN!
WAIT...
...WHERE IS HE?
HE... HE'S BEING BRAVE NOW.
AND WE HAVE TO GO...
FOLLOW ALONG.
WWWZZZT
THERE IT IS-- THE NEXT GATE.
YES...

HURRY AND ACTIVATE THE GATE!
WE WON'T HAVE MUCH TIME BEFORE THEY'RE...
HERE.
NO... OH NO...
HELLO, CHILDREN.
WE HAVE ENJOYED THIS GAME.
BUT NOW IT IS TIME.
YOU WILL JOIN US.

DAMMIT...
WHAT DO WE DO?

ACTIVATE THE GATE...

THOOOM
FORTY SECONDS...

YAAARRHH!

WAIT...
FORTY SECONDS...

KKKHHHSSSHHHH
THERE.

KKSSHHSSHH-DOOM
IT'S... ME...
FORTY SECONDS...

HAHAHAHAHAHA
PAAAAAAAARK!
GO GO GO!
GAAAHHHH!
NO!

KKSHHHSSHHH
THREE!
COME ON!
PLEASE...

OH...
THIS IS NEW...
YEAH...

WHOA...
QI QI
WHAT IS THIS?
IT... DOESN'T EVEN MAKE SENSE.
IT'S NOT EVEN A WORLD.
JUST *FLOATING* OUT HERE... IN SPACE...
THIS IS THE HOTEL AT THE EDGE OF THE UNIVERSE.
IT'S THE END.
HOW DO YOU KNOW THAT?
BECAUSE I'VE BEEN HERE BEFORE.

TWO... WAIT.
PLEASE-- WE NEED YOU TO EXPLAIN.
THIS IS THE FINAL GATE.
WE JUST HAVE TO HOPE THAT WE BOUGHT OURSELVES ENOUGH TIME...
THIS IS THEIR PLACE-- THE HORDE. THEY NEVER WENT ON.
THERE'S SOMETHING HERE-- SOMETHING THAT INFECTED THEM-- MADE THEM THE WAY THEY ARE.
THEY...THEY WORSHIP IT.
WHY ARE THEY STILL HERE? WHY HAVEN'T THEY USED THE FINAL GATE?
I DON'T KNOW. BUT IT'S NOT GOOD.
THEY--
THOOOM
DAMMIT... THEY'RE ALREADY BACK.
WE HAVE TO GO. NOW.

OH...
WAIT... WHAT IS THAT?
OH, HELL...
THAT TREE...IT'S LIKE THE ONE ON THE JUNGLE WORLD.
BIGGER, BUT...
DAMMIT...

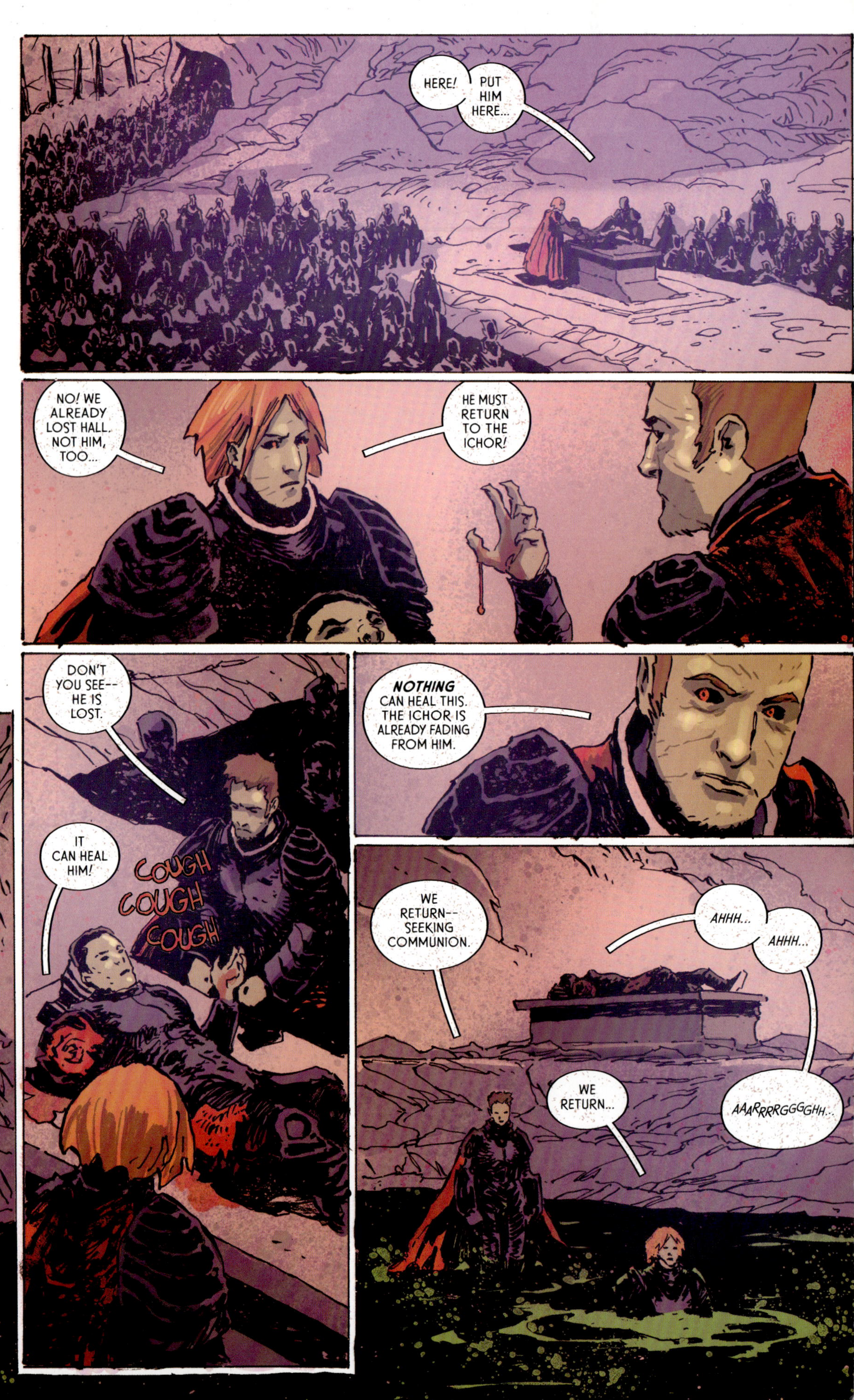
HERE!
PUT HIM HERE...
NO! WE ALREADY LOST HALL. NOT HIM, TOO...
HE MUST RETURN TO THE ICHOR!
DON'T YOU SEE-- HE IS LOST.
IT CAN HEAL HIM!
COUGH COUGH COUGH
NOTHING CAN HEAL THIS. THE ICHOR IS ALREADY FADING FROM HIM.
WE RETURN-- SEEKING COMMUNION.
AHHH...
AHHH...
WE RETURN...
AAARRRRGGGGHH...

WE HAVE TO GO NOW.
THIS IS OUR ONLY CHANCE.
THIS WAY NOW.
OKAY...
I THINK IT'S CLEAR.

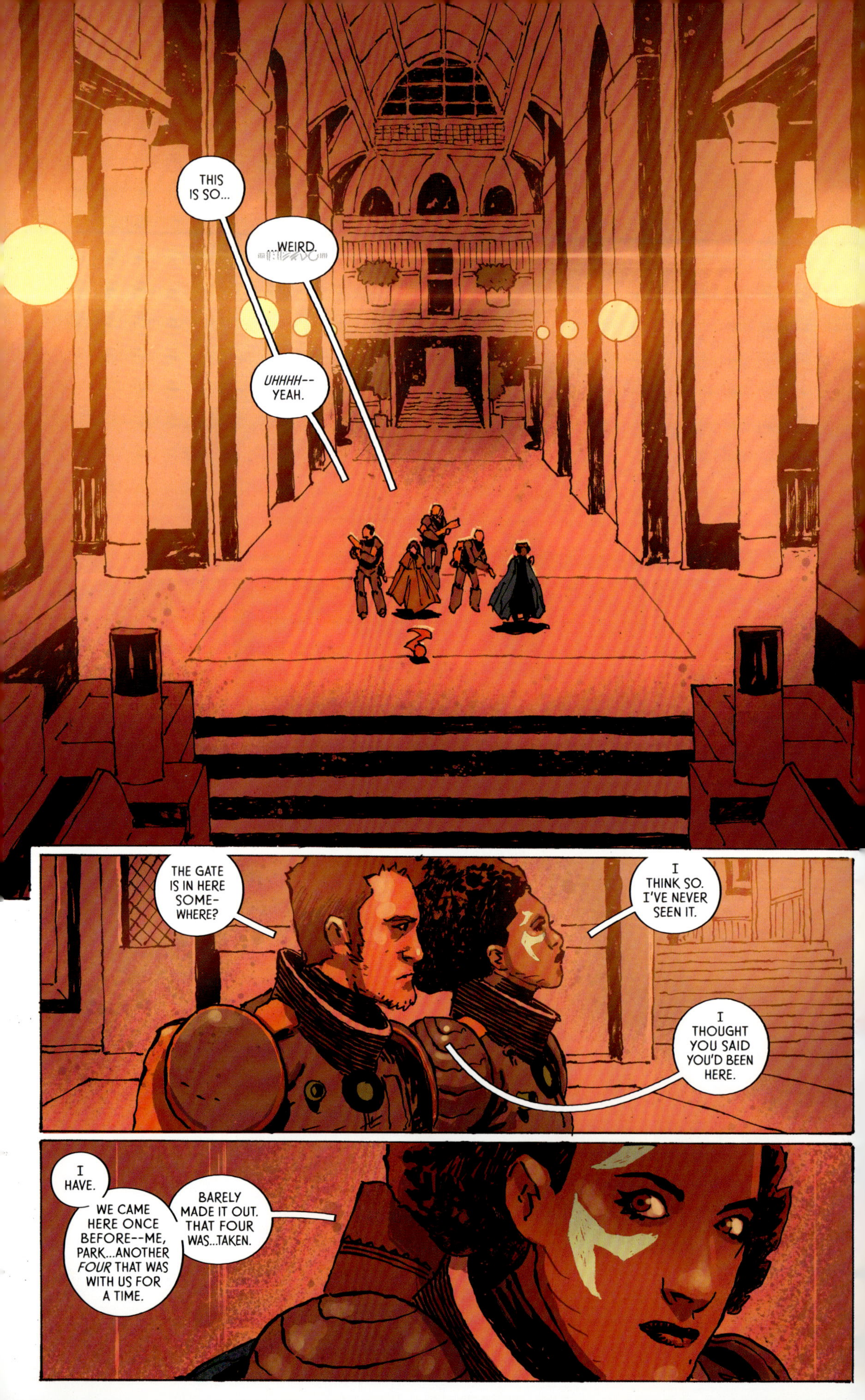

THIS IS SO...
...WEIRD.
UHHHH--YEAH.
THE GATE IS IN HERE SOMEWHERE?
I THINK SO. I'VE NEVER SEEN IT.
I THOUGHT YOU SAID YOU'D BEEN HERE.
I HAVE.
WE CAME HERE ONCE BEFORE--ME, PARK...ANOTHER *FOUR* THAT WAS WITH US FOR A TIME.
BARELY MADE IT OUT. THAT FOUR WAS...TAKEN.

SIGNAL IS...REALLY STRANGE HERE.
WE STILL MIGHT BE ABLE TO CONNECT TO THE GATE, THOUGH.
TRY.

TiNG

IT'S LOCKING ON TO THE GATE.
TiNG

ALL RIGHT. LET'S FIND THIS THING AND GET THE HELL OUT OF HERE.

TiNG

TING
HEY...
YOU KNOW WHAT THAT WAS BACK DOWN THERE.
THAT THING, BY THE TREE...
THAT--THAT LOOKED LIKE SOME KIND OF...BOMB.
I DON'T EVEN...I MEAN... THEY'RE DOING *SOMETHING* WITH THAT.
WHICH IS WHY WE HAVE TO GO NOW.
ABSOLUTELY.
BUT WE DON'T KNOW WHAT THE HELL THEY'RE DOING WITH THAT THING.
ALL I KNOW IS THAT THEY HAVE AN ARMY AND THE GATES.
AND NOW, A BIG-ASS *BOMB.*
AAAHHH!

GAIA!

IT'S OKAY, GAIA.
THEY CAN'T HARM YOU.
THEY'RE SHADOWS.
GHOSTS.
COME ON.
WE'VE GOT A LOCK ON THE GATE.
HAVE YOU SEEN THE SPACEMAN?
HE'S COMING SOON.
HERALDS ITS GREAT RETURN. FROM THE ROOTS.

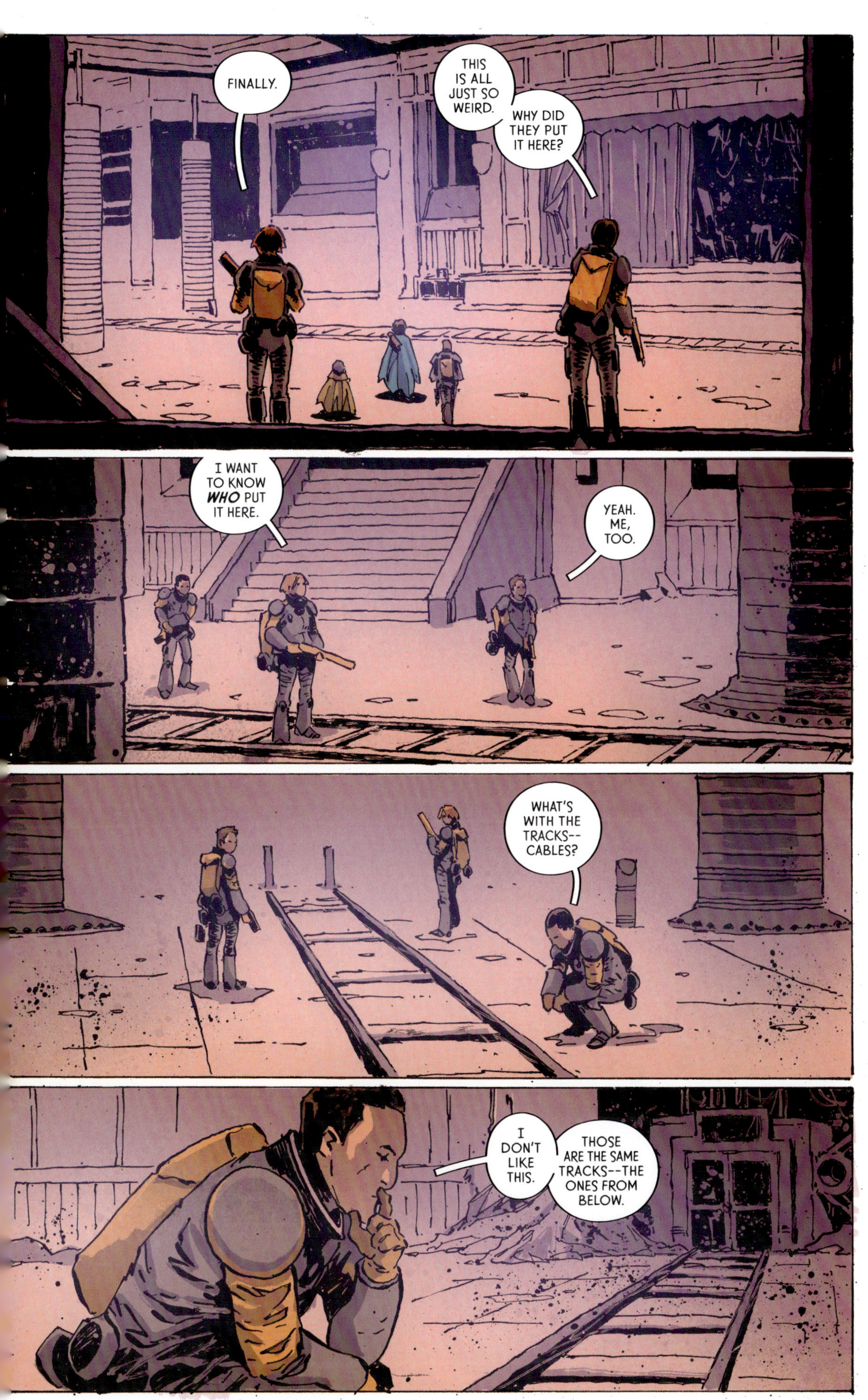
FINALLY.
THIS IS ALL JUST SO WEIRD.
WHY DID THEY PUT IT HERE?
I WANT TO KNOW **WHO** PUT IT HERE.
YEAH. ME, TOO.
WHAT'S WITH THE TRACKS--CABLES?
I DON'T LIKE THIS.
THOSE ARE THE SAME TRACKS--THE ONES FROM BELOW.

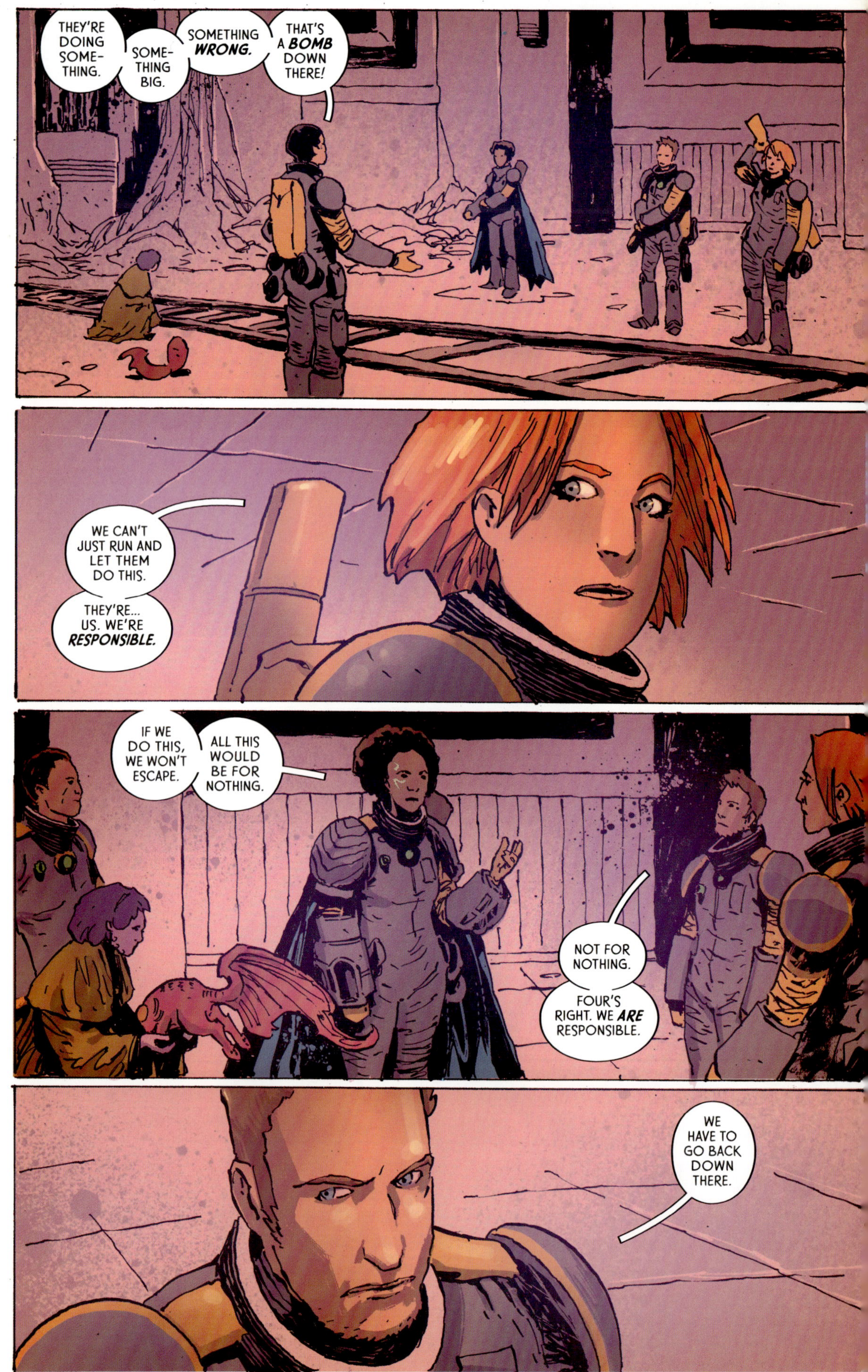
THEY'RE DOING SOME-THING.
SOME-THING BIG.
SOMETHING WRONG.
THAT'S A BOMB DOWN THERE!
WE CAN'T JUST RUN AND LET THEM DO THIS.
THEY'RE... US. WE'RE RESPONSIBLE.
IF WE DO THIS, WE WON'T ESCAPE.
ALL THIS WOULD BE FOR NOTHING.
NOT FOR NOTHING.
FOUR'S RIGHT. WE ARE RESPONSIBLE.
WE HAVE TO GO BACK DOWN THERE.

LITTLE CLONES...
N-NUMBERS FOR NAMES...
COUGH COUGH COUGH

THEY... SLUMBER WITHIN THE ICHOR.
IF NOT... IF THEY COULD HEAR YOU, YOU WOULD BE OURS.

COME CLOSER. LET ME SEE HOW I...ONCE WAS.
I-I'M DYING.
THE ICHOR HAS-HAS LEFT ME...

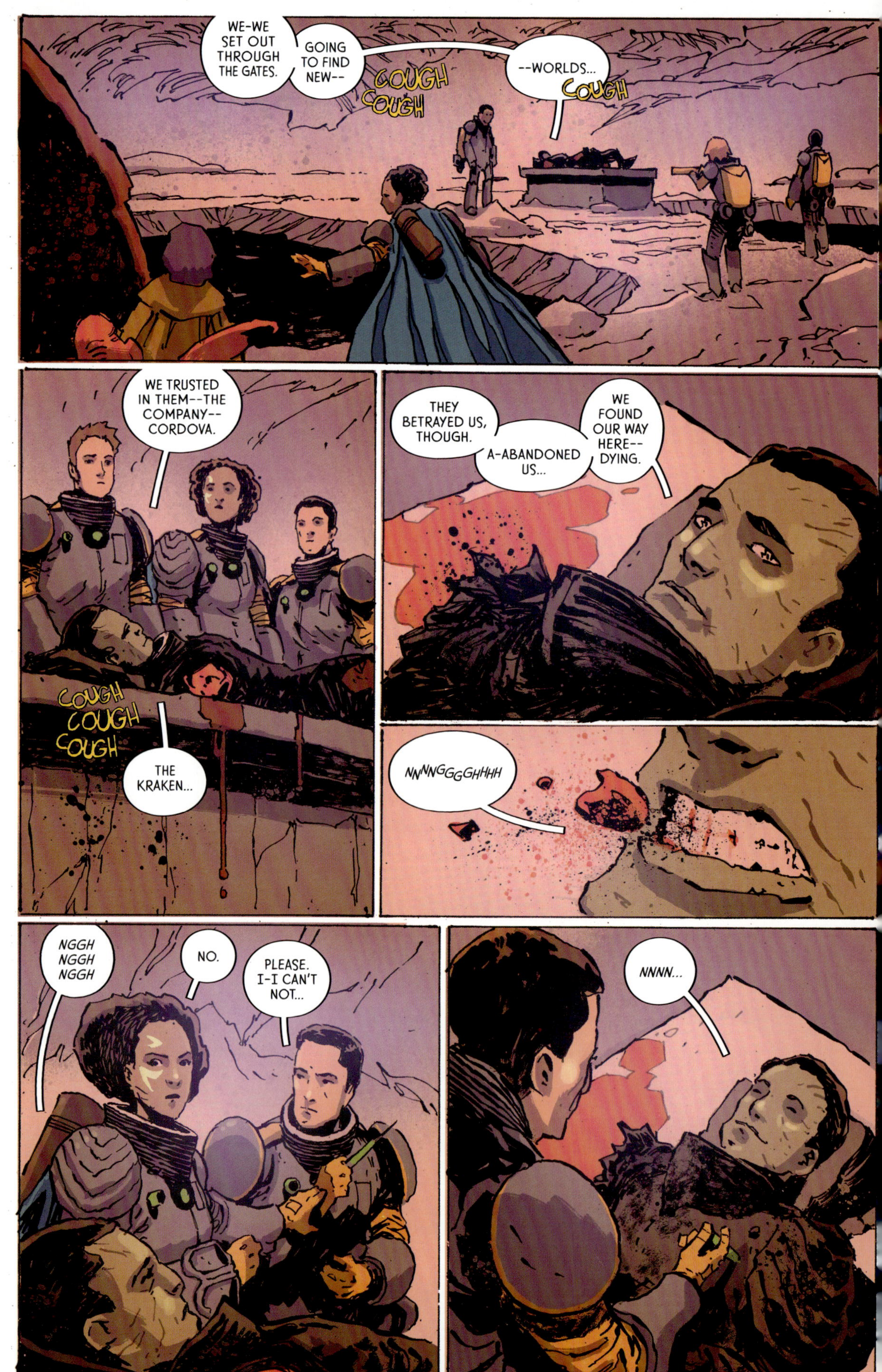
WE-WE SET OUT THROUGH THE GATES.
GOING TO FIND NEW--
COUGH COUGH
--WORLDS...
COUGH
WE TRUSTED IN THEM--THE COMPANY--CORDOVA.
COUGH COUGH COUGH
THE KRAKEN...
THEY BETRAYED US, THOUGH.
A-ABANDONED US...
WE FOUND OUR WAY HERE--DYING.
NNNNGGGGHHHH
NGGH NGGH NGGH
NO.
PLEASE. I-I CAN'T NOT...
NNNN...

THANK YOU.
I-I HAVEN'T FELT PAIN IN...SO LONG.
A PIECE OF AN OLD GOD-- THE ROOT FELL HERE. THE DARK TREE GREW FROM THAT.
IT-IT INFECTED US. CH-CHANGED...
WE WERE BETRAYED. ABANDONED. DERANGED...
SO WE TOOK EVERYTHING-- BECAME A PLAGUE--THE HORDE.
WHAT ABOUT THAT? THE BOMB?
WHAT ARE YOU DOING WITH IT?
HEH... HEH...OH, THAT...
THAT IS THE END. OF EVERYTHING.
GATE POWERS... THE BOMB.
IF IT DETONATES IN-INSIDE THE G-GATE AS IT JUMPS...
...IT WILL TEAR THROUGH ALL THE GATES. ALL THE WORLDS... AT ONCE.
YOU CAN'T LET THEM...LET... US...

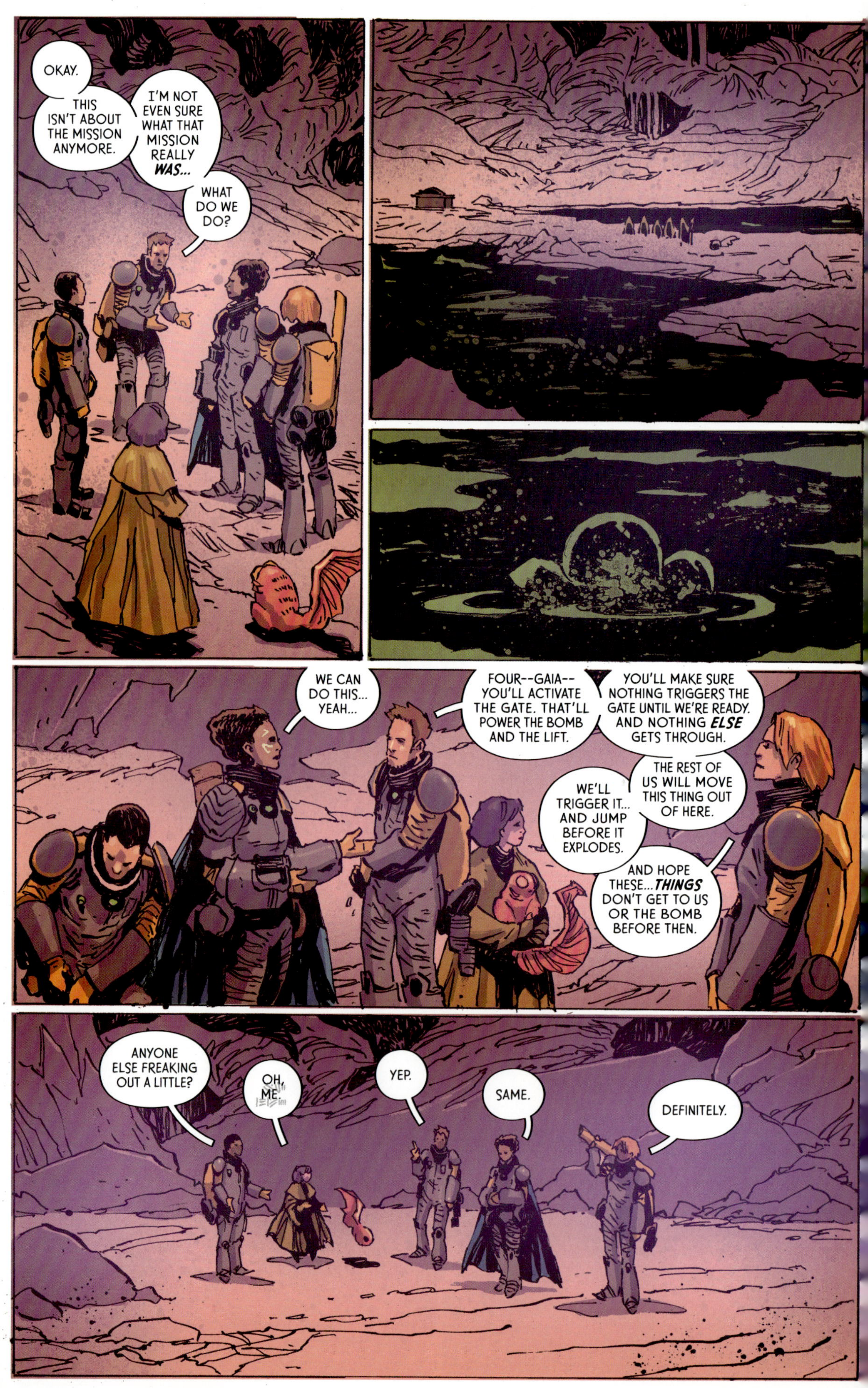
OKAY.
THIS ISN'T ABOUT THE MISSION ANYMORE.
I'M NOT EVEN SURE WHAT THAT MISSION REALLY *WAS...*
WHAT DO WE DO?
WE CAN DO THIS... YEAH...
FOUR--GAIA-- YOU'LL ACTIVATE THE GATE. THAT'LL POWER THE BOMB AND THE LIFT.
YOU'LL MAKE SURE NOTHING TRIGGERS THE GATE UNTIL WE'RE READY. AND NOTHING *ELSE* GETS THROUGH.
THE REST OF US WILL MOVE THIS THING OUT OF HERE.
WE'LL TRIGGER IT... AND JUMP BEFORE IT EXPLODES.
AND HOPE THESE... *THINGS* DON'T GET TO US OR THE BOMB BEFORE THEN.
ANYONE ELSE FREAKING OUT A LITTLE?
OH, ME.
YEP.
SAME.
DEFINITELY.

DO YOU S-STILL LOVE HER? FOUR?
EVEN AFTER ALL THESE GENERATIONS?
I DO.

OKAY.
DO IT.

THOOOM
FORTY SECONDS...

YES.

THOOOM

GO GO GO!
THOOOM

FORTY SECONDS...
THOOOM

THOOOM

THOOOM

THOOOM
HURRY! THEY'RE COMING.

THOOOM

THOOOM

FORTY SECONDS...
GO!
HURRY!
I AM, DAMMIT!
WHAT'VE YOU DONE, YOU FOOL?
WHAT'S RIGHT...
TIK
DOOM
HOLY...

NO!
I AM GAIA... OF THE PROTECTORATE. LAST OF MY KIND.
I STAND SO THAT OTHERS CAN LIVE.
I STAND...
YAAAHH!
HAHAHAHA!

NNNNGHH
RRRHHH
GAH!
NUFF
FWIP
RRAAAHH!
NNNNNN

SHNNK
GAIA!
FOUR!
THREE--
CHECK ON
HER.
THE REST
OF YOU HELP
ME GET THIS
THING IN
PLACE!
WE DON'T
HAVE MUCH
TIME...
WH-WHAT
HAPPENED?
SHE'S
GONNA BE
OKAY!
BZZZT
ONE! WHAT
THE HELL IS
GOING ON?
YOU
GOTTA BE
KIDDING
ME.
WHAT--
BZZZT
--YOU MEAN?
WE NEED A
REPORT,
NOW!

SHUT THE HELL UP!
WHAT...
WE KNOW. ABOUT EVERYTHING.
WHAT YOU'VE DONE TO US. WHAT WE *ARE.*
IT STOPS. NOW.
THIS STOPS NOTHING.
WE'RE COMING.
HEH. YEAH, WE'LL SEE ABOUT THAT.
WE--
BEEP
WE GO NOW!
ONE! THE DELAY?
I'VE GOT IT! *GO!*
I'LL ACTIVATE THE BOMB LAST SECOND--JUMP BEFORE IT CLOSES.
GO! PLEASE!
DON'T SCREW THIS UP.
YEAH.

YEAH...
KSSSSHHH
RAAAAHHHH
THOOOM
YOOOOOOOOU!
SLAM
WAAANNNN
WAAANNNNN
NOOOOO!
WAAANNNNN
RAAAAHHHH
WAAANNNNN

YOU'VE COME SO FAR...
...AFTER ALL THIS TIME.

WE SENT OUT THE MESSAGE--
--SO VERY LONG AGO.
WE SENT OUT THE CALL AND OPENED THE GATES TOO LATE.
THINGS WENT SO **VERY** WRONG.
WE NEEDED YOU THEN.
WE NEED YOU **EVEN MORE** NOW.
HOW CAN WE HELP?
AN END. AND A BEGINNING...

JEREMY HAUN, writer and cocreator of *40 Seconds*, has worked for nearly every major publisher in the comics industry. He has drawn projects including *Batwoman* and *Constantine* for DC Comics. He has also written and drawn several creator-owned projects, including *The Beauty* and *The Realm* for Image Comics and *The Red Mother* for Boom! Studios. Jeremy resides in a crumbling mansion in Joplin, Missouri, with his family and a terrible orange cat. He can be found online at @jerhaun and Patreon.com/JeremyHaun.

CHRISTOPHER MITTEN, artist and cocreator of *40 Seconds*, is originally from the cow-dappled expanse of southern Wisconsin. He now spends his time roaming the misty wilds of suburban Chicago, drawing little people in little boxes. Among others, he has contributed work for Dark Horse, DC Comics, Oni Press, Vertigo, Image Comics, Marvel Comics, IDW, Black Mask, Gallery Books, Titan Comics, 44FLOOD, and Simon & Schuster. He can be found online at ChristopherMitten.com and on Instagram at @Chris_Mitten.

BRETT WELDELE is an Eisner-nominated comics creator living in Portland, Oregon. Recent projects include the Kickstarters for *One Fall* and *Starlite*, as well as *The Surrogates* (Top Shelf), *Pariah* (Dark Horse), *Ultimate Spider-Man* (Marvel), *Vampirella 1969* (Dynamite), *Halloween* (Devil's Due), *Se7en* (Zenescope), and *Southland Tales* (Graphitti Designs). Brett's watercolor prints can be found at BrettWeldele.PatternByEtsy.com and on Instagram at @brettweldele.

THOMAS MAUER has lent his lettering and design talent to numerous critically acclaimed and award-winning projects since the early 2000s. Among his recent work are AfterShock Comics' *Godkillers* and *Miles to Go*, Comixology's *In the Flood* and *The Dark*, and Image Comics' *Hardcore* and *The Realm*. You can follow him on Twitter at @thomasmauer and see samples of his work at ThomasMauer.com.